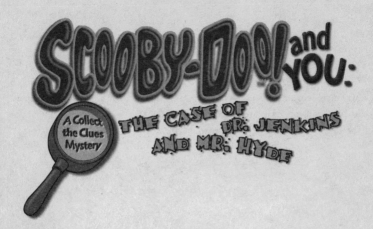

SCOOBY-DOO! and YOU:

A Collect the Clues Mystery

THE CASE OF DR. JENKINS AND MR. HYDE

By James Gelsey

SCHOLASTIC INC.
New York   Toronto   London   Auckland   Sydney
Mexico City   New Delhi   Hong Kong

No part of this publication may be reproduced in whole or in part, or stored in a retrieval system, or transmitted in any form or by any means, electronic, mechanical, photocopying, recording, or otherwise, without written permission of the publisher. For information regarding permission, write to Scholastic Inc., Attention: Permissions Dept., 555 Broadway, New York, NY 10012.

ISBN 0-439-23157-4

Copyright © 2001 by Hanna-Barbera.
SCOOBY-DOO and all related characters and elements are trademarks of
Hanna-Barbera © 2001.
CARTOON NETWORK and logo are trademarks of
Cartoon Network © 2001.
All rights reserved. Published by Scholastic Inc.,
555 Broadway, New York, NY 10012.
SCHOLASTIC and associated logos are trademarks
and/or registered trademarks of Scholastic Inc.

12 11 10 9   5 6/0

Cover and interior illustrations by Duendes del Sur
Cover and interior design by Madalina Stefan

Printed in the U.S.A.

First Scholastic printing, March 2001

It's a windy day as you ride your bicycle down the street. You're looking for 33⅓ Kendall Street. You've been up and down the street four or five times already and can't seem to find it. Then, as you're about to give up, you notice a small wooden sign swinging over an alley.

"Thirty-three and a third," you read. You get off your bike and slowly walk into the alley.

The sounds of dishes clanking and people talking fills the air. When you reach the other end, the alley opens up onto a large courtyard. You lean your bicycle against the wall and hear someone call your name. You look up and see Daphne waving to you.

"Hi, everyone," you smile as you walk over to the gang. They're all sitting around a big round table.

"Here, we saved a seat for you," Fred says, gesturing to an empty seat next to Scooby-Doo.

"Hey, Scooby," you say as you sit down next to him. Scooby doesn't seem to hear you. He and Shaggy are studying the menu very, very closely.

"I don't think we have anything to worry about, Scoob," Shaggy announces. "Doesn't look like there's any Yummaroni and Cheese here."

"That's right, mate," the waiter says. "Only fish 'n' chips here at Nigel Ruddigore's. So what'll it be then? Fish 'n' chips all around?"

"Sounds good to me," Shaggy answers.

"Everything sounds good to you," Velma says. "Everything but —"

"Like, don't say it, Velma," Shaggy moans.

You get a puzzled look on your face.

"Let me explain," Fred says. "Our last mystery was so strange, it even made Shaggy and Scooby lose their appetites."

"Would you like to read about it?" Daphne asks.

"You can even try to solve the mystery yourself," Velma adds.

Fred takes a small notebook out of his pocket and hands it to you.

"Here's our Clue Keeper," he says. "It was my turn to keep notes, so I did my best to make sure everything that happened was written down."

"As you read our notebook, keep your own Clue Keeper handy," Daphne suggests. "That way, you'll be able to jot down the clues and suspects you find."

"Remember, 👁 👁 means you've met a suspect, and a 🔍 shows you a clue," Velma explains. "And we'll even help you out along the way."

"So enjoy the Clue Keeper," Fred says. "And good luck solving *The Case of Dr. Jenkins and Mr. Hyde!*"

Clue Keeper Entry 1

"Stop the van!" Shaggy shouted. I pulled off the road and slammed on the brakes.

"What is it, Shaggy?" I asked. "Is everything okay?"

"Didn't you see that sign back there?" Shaggy said.

"Which one? Is there a detour on the road?" Velma asked.

"No, the sign about the Yummaroni and Cheese," Shaggy said.

"What are you talking about, Shaggy?" Daphne asked. "We're supposed to be going to the movies."

"How can you even think about movies at a time like this?" pleaded Shaggy.

"A time like what?" Velma asked.

"Like, a time like this where they're giving away free food!" exclaimed Shaggy. "Look over there!"

Set back from the road we saw a large white building. A large red-and-yellow tent stood next to it. We could see balloons and flags waving in the wind.

"I think that's the headquarters of Yummy Foods," Velma said. "I seem to remember reading about them in the newspaper. They must be launching their new macaroni and cheese product today."

"And we wouldn't want to miss an historical occasion like that, right?" asked Shaggy.

"*Right!*" agreed Scooby.

"Okay, you two," I said. "We'll only stop long enough for you to get a quick sample. Then it's off to the movies."

"Thanks, Fred, old pal," Shaggy said.

I steered the Mystery Machine back onto

the road and headed toward the balloons and the big red-and-yellow tent. A lot of cars were already there. A huge, red-and-yellow YUMMARONI AND CHEESE banner covered one side of the big, white building. We all got out of the van and walked over to the tent. A tall man wearing a white lab coat was greeting people.

"Hey, there!" he said happily. "Welcome to Yummy Foods! I'm Dr. Lavoris Jenkins, the president and chief foodologist here at Yummy Foods."

"Nice to meet you," I replied. "I'm Fred. And this is Velma, Daphne, Shaggy, and Scooby-Doo."

"Help yourself to any of Yummy Foods' world-famous products," Dr. Jenkins offered. "And don't miss the official first taste of Yummaroni and Cheese, with my secret ingredient that brings out the best in you!"

A man walked up to Dr.

Jenkins and handed him a piece of paper. Dr. Jenkins frowned as he read it.

"Is everything all right, Dr. Jenkins?" Daphne asked.

"What? Oh, yes, yes, everything's fine," he replied. "Just another threatening e-mail from someone named 'Mr. Hyde.'"

"May we take a look at it?" I asked.

Dr. Jenkins handed me the paper. "'This

is your last warning to stop production of Yummaroni,'" I read out loud. "'Otherwise, I'll make sure your first bite brings out the *beast* in you.'"

"Jinkies," Velma said.

"I'm sure you've got nothing to worry about, sir," I assured him.

"Except maybe them," said a man in a white lab coat as he walked over to us. He

pointed to Shaggy and Scooby. They were inside the nearby tent, filling their plates with food from the "free samples" tables. "They'll eat up all of your profits, Dr. Jenkins."

We all laughed.

"You'd better be getting back to the lab, Nebbins," Dr. Jenkins said. "And I'd better return to welcoming our other guests. Have fun, kids." Dr. Jenkins walked back toward the front of the building.

"Ah-ah-ah-ah-CHOO!"

"Gesundheit," Daphne said.

"Thank you," the man replied, taking a white handkerchief from his pocket. "I'm Wally Nebbins. Please pardon my sneezing. Must be my allergies. I'm not used to being outside. I'm usually locked away in the food lab, working on secret ingredients."

"Like the one Dr. Jenkins created for the Yummaroni and Cheese?" I asked.

"You mean, the one I created," Wally said angrily.

The gang and I exchanged glances. An unhappy employee always tells us we've found a possible suspect. And Wally Nebbins seemed very unhappy.

"I'm the chief food scientist here," he continued. "I'm the one who made Yummy Crunchies so crunchy, Yummy Snacks so tangy, and now Yummaroni and Cheese so . . . so . . . yummy! I've worked here for years only to see Dr. Jenkins take all the credit. And I'm tired of it. Now if you'll excuse me, I have to go back inside."

Wally Nebbins kept sneezing as he walked toward the big, white building. Suddenly, a crashing sound came from one corner of the tent.

"Jinkies!" exclaimed Velma. "What was that?" Daphne, Velma, and I looked at one another. "Shaggy and Scooby!" we said together.

"Let's go see what happened," I said.

Velma's Mystery-Solving Tips

"Jinkies! We just arrived and we already learned about a potential mystery and met a suspect. Did you see the 👁 👁 on page 10? Now's when you should take out a pencil and your own Clue Keeper. Jot down your answers to these questions, and then read on."

1. What is the suspect's name?

2. What does he do at Yummy Foods?

3. Why is he angry at Dr. Jenkins?

Clue Keeper Entry 2

By the time we got inside the tent, a small crowd had already gathered. We made our way through and found Shaggy and Scooby sitting on the ground. An upended table lay beside them. A huge pile of packages, bottles, and containers had rolled in every direction.

"Hi, guys," Shaggy said with a smile. "Like, what's up?"

"Certainly not that table," Velma said. "What happened?"

"It was an accident," Shaggy explained, standing up. "Scoob and I were trying to reach the last box of Yummy Crunchies when the table gave out from under us."

"You mean you were standing on the table?" Daphne asked.

"Sure," Shaggy said. "The last box was hanging by a string from the top of the tent."

"Shaggy, that was just a display box," I explained. "You're not supposed to take those."

"What's going on here?" someone yelled. A man in a white jumpsuit and ball cap pushed his way through the crowd. "Holy macaroni!" he exclaimed when he saw the mess. He knelt down and started picking up boxes. Then he stopped and looked around at the crowd. "Who did this?"

Shaggy and Scooby slowly raised their hands.

"Well, don't just stand there," the man ordered. "Help me get this mess cleaned up!"

Shaggy and Scooby jumped into action and helped gather up all the boxes, bags, and other packages of food. As Scooby picked up a plastic bottle, some kind of clear liquid dripped all over him. He took a couple of sniffs.

"*Reeeeeech!*" he said, holding his nose. He quickly dropped the bottle.

"Like, sorry about the mess, man," Shaggy said.

"My name's Izzy Fenwick, not 'man,'" the man said. He suddenly looked around, sniffing the air. "Where is that smell coming from?" He followed the smell to Scooby. "Smells to me like you've got some of our Yummy Vinegar on you," he said as he wiped off Scooby's back with a white rag. He stuffed the rag into his pocket.

"*Ranks!*" Scooby said, giving the man a lick across the face.

"Now that's what I call a 'thank you,'" Izzy

Fenwick said. "You're about the only folks around here who have shown me any respect. Fact of the matter is, no one really has any respect for the janitor."

Just at that moment, Dr. Jenkins walked by.

"Nonsense, Izzy," said Dr. Jenkins. "I think you're doing a fine job. You're a credit to the Yummy Foods' team. Here, have a pen." He handed Izzy a red-and-yellow pen. "What do you think? They're going to be part of the promotion."

"It's a pen," Izzy said, looking at it.

"Open the top," Dr. Jenkins said. Izzy took the top off and quickly put it back on again.

"What was that smell?" he asked.

"It's a Yummaroni-and-Cheese-scented pen," Dr. Jenkins said with a big smile. "I've only made two of these so far, so keep it out of sight. I don't want people to make a mad rush for them."

"Don't worry, sir," Izzy said. "Your secret is safe with me."

Dr. Jenkins continued on his way.

"For fifteen years I've worked here, and that's the most he's ever said to me," Izzy complained. "But what really angers me is this Yummaroni and Cheese thing. They've been working on it for years. Experimenting with different cheeses and whatnot."

"That sounds interesting," Daphne says.

"Yeah, it's interesting unless you have to clean it up every night," Izzy said. "They've actually had cheese explode all over the laboratory! Have you ever tried to clean gooey cheese out of a light socket? It's not fun. I'd be very happy if this whole Yummaroni and Cheese thing disappeared. I don't think I can stand one more night of cleaning up after Yummaroni and Cheese."

Izzy walked away and I looked at my watch.

"If we're going to catch the movie, we'd better get going soon," I said.

"But Scooby and I haven't gotten our taste of Yummaroni and Cheese," Shaggy complained. "Just a few more minutes. And then we can leave."

"*Reeeeeeeease?*" begged Scooby.

"Do you two think you can stay out of trouble for five more minutes?" Velma asked.

"*Riece of rake,*" Scooby replied.

"He means piece of *Yummy* Cake," Shaggy added with a smile.

Daphne's Mystery-Solving Tips

"Did you see 👁 👁 on page 16? That means you met our second suspect. Answer these questions about him in your Clue Keeper."

1. What is the suspect's name?

2. What is his connection to Yummy Foods?

3. Why do you think he could be a suspect?

"Once you're done, keep reading our Clue Keeper to see what happened next."

Clue Keeper Entry 3

We followed Shaggy and Scooby to the big YUMMARONI AND CHEESE sign at the far end of the tent. The sign was hanging over a large stage. There was a podium with the Yummy Foods logo on the left side of the stage. A long table with six chairs behind it stood next to the podium.

"Is it me, or do the table and chairs look a little small to you?" Daphne said.

"That's because they're kiddie-sized," a woman said behind us. We turned and saw a woman dressed in a business suit. "They're going to invite some kids for the official tasting," she continued. "It's really good publicity."

"Oh, are you in charge of publicity for Yummy Foods?" I asked.

"I used to be," she answered. "Until my uncle decided not to give me a promotion. That's when I left and started working for another food company. I'm Katherine. Katherine Jenkins Tatum." 👁 👁

"Katherine *Jenkins* Tatum?" Velma asked. "Are you related to Dr. Jenkins?"

"That's right," she replied with a smile. "He's my uncle. Listen, my company is starting our own line of macaroni foods. I'll write down our address and you can come to our special tasting day." She fished in her purse, looking for a pen.

Dr. Jenkins ran over to us. His eyes were fixed on his niece. "What are you doing here, K. J.?"

"Just thought I'd pay a visit to my favorite uncle," she answered.

"Seems to me you're here to spy on your favorite uncle," Dr. Jenkins said. "You'd better leave, K. J. I don't want to have to call security."

"Fine. Just let me write down some information for these kids, and I'll be on my way," K. J. replied. As Dr. Jenkins looked around for security, K. J. plucked a pen from the pocket of his white jacket. "Just what I was looking for," she said as she wrote quickly on a slip of paper.

Dr. Jenkins spotted a security guard by the tent doorway and charged off to get him.

"Pardon us for asking, but why would he have to call security for his own niece?" Daphne asked.

"Because I happen to be the head of So-Good Foods," K. J. replied matter-of-factly.

"But So-Good Foods and Yummy Foods are rivals!" Daphne exclaimed.

"Jinkies, it must be strange to compete against your uncle," Velma said.

"I don't like it, but his success can affect my business," K. J. said, still looking in her purse. "We've been racing to get our macaroni line out first, but he's beaten us. The fact is that if Yummaroni and Cheese really

takes off, my company will be in big trouble. But I'd better run now before I get into big trouble. I hope you kids can come to our tasting."

K. J. Tatum walked away and disappeared into the crowd.

"Hey, where are Shaggy and Scooby?" Velma asked. We looked around, but didn't see them anywhere.

"Here we go again!" I exclaimed. We started to look for them when Dr. Jenkins's voice boomed through the tent.

"Ladies and gentlemen, may I have your attention please?"

We looked up and saw Dr. Jenkins standing behind the podium on the stage.

"Thank you all for coming today," he said. "We are thrilled you are here to witness the introduction of Yummy Foods' newest product, Yummaroni and Cheese!"

Everyone clapped as balloons and confetti fell from the top of the tent.

"To get things started, we've invited our official taste testers to help us out," he continued. "Please give them a big hand!"

Four children walked up onto the platform and sat down behind the table. They were wearing red-and-yellow shirts that said either "Yummaroni" or "Cheese."

"Oh, brother!" exclaimed Velma. "Look!"

We watched as Shaggy and Scooby walked onto the stage. They were wearing the shirts, too, and they sat down on the remaining two kiddie chairs.

"Now I've seen everything!" Daphne said.

"**W**ell, it looks like you've met another suspect, right? Check out the 👀 on page 22, open your Clue Keeper, and then answer these questions."

1. What is the suspect's name?

2. What is the suspect's connection to Yummy Foods?

3. Why do you think she could be behind the mysterious e-mails?

"After you've written down your answers, check out entry 4."

27

Clue Keeper Entry 4

"Now, before we let our official taste testers take their official tastes," Dr. Jenkins began, "I'd like to show you something." He reached into the podium and took out a bowl of orange powder.

"This, my friends, is the Yummaroni and Cheese secret ingredient," he announced. "This special combination of cheeses and other wonderful flavors make Yummaroni and Cheese absolutely delicious and completely irresistible. Now let's get ready to eat!"

He put the bowl on top of the podium. Two men in white lab coats walked onstage and placed a bowl of Yummaroni and Cheese and a spoon in front of each kid and Shaggy and Scooby. They left boxes of it on the table, as well. One of the men handed Dr. Jenkins a bowl and spoon, too.

"Okay, everyone, get ready!" Dr. Jenkins said with a smile. He raised his spoon up in the air. Everyone at the tasting table did that, too. "One. Two. Three!"

Scooby, Shaggy, and the kids started eating their Yummaroni and Cheese. Shaggy and Scooby couldn't seem to eat it fast enough.

"You know what, Scoob?" Shaggy said between bites. "Like, this really is absolutely delicious."

We all watched as Dr. Jenkins took a spoonful of Yummaroni and Cheese and put it into his mouth. Suddenly, he started coughing. He grabbed his throat and then fell down behind the podium. He must have knocked the bowl of orange powder, because there was a huge explosion of orange smoke and dust. When it cleared, Dr. Jenkins slowly stood up again. Only it wasn't Dr. Jenkins.

"Zoinks!" Shaggy exclaimed. "It's-it's-it's-it's-a-a —"

"*Ronster!*" Scooby yelled.

"It's Mr. Hyde!" Daphne exclaimed.

An angry and wild-looking monster-man stood behind the podium. Shaggy and Scooby dived under the table. The other kids ran off the stage to their parents.

"Where's Dr. Jenkins?" someone shouted from the audience.

"I *was* Dr. Jenkins," he growled. "Now

Dr. Jenkins is gone forever and Mr. Hyde is here in his place! I've put my own secret ingredient into the Yummaroni and Cheese."

He held up a small container of blue liquid. "Once I start the food production line, anyone who eats Yummaroni and Cheese will turn into a monster like me!"

There was another burst of orange powder!

When it cleared, the monster was gone!

Everyone in the tent screamed as they ran back to their cars.

"You know, there's something strange about this," Velma said.

"Velma's right," I agreed. "I think we should take a look around."

We walked onto the stage and saw a paw come out from under the tablecloth. It felt around the table top until it came to an unfinished box of Yummaroni and Cheese. Another paw came up. Then the two paws grabbed the box and brought it under the tablecloth.

Daphne went over to the table and lifted up the cloth. Shaggy and Scooby were eating the Yummaroni and Cheese.

"No sense in letting it go to waste," Shaggy explained.

I knelt down behind the podium to look for clues. I saw something sticking out of the powder. It was one of the Yummaroni-and-Cheese-scented red-and-yellow pens that Dr. Jenkins had created.

"Something tells me that we'll find more of them inside the factory," Velma said. "There's a trail of orange powder that goes from under the stage to the factory. There must be a trap door near the podium that leads under the stage."

"Then let's not waste any time," I said. "We've got a mystery to solve."

Scooby and Shaggy's
Mystery-Solving Tips

"Like, I'll bet you noticed that  on page 33, right? It's pretty important. Open up your Clue Keeper and answer these questions about it. Then keep on reading to learn what we discovered inside the factory."

1. What is the clue?

2. How do you think the clue could have gotten there?

3. Which of the suspects do you think could have left this clue?

Clue Keeper Entry 5

We followed the trail of orange powder to a side door of the factory. The door was slightly open. We walked inside and saw one flight of stairs going up and one going down.

"It looks like the orange trail ends here," Velma noticed.

"So I guess that means we have to go home," Shaggy said hopefully.

Suddenly, we heard the sound of a door slamming and footsteps coming up the stairs.

"Mr. Fenwick, you startled us," Daphne said.

"What are you kids doing in here?" he asked.

"Uh, Shaggy and Scooby just needed to wash up," I said. "Dr. Jenkins said it was okay."

"Well, be quick," Izzy Fenwick said. "The bathrooms are at the top of the stairs. I'm going start cleaning things up in the tent." He went outside and walked toward the tent.

"He'll be back soon, so we'd better work quickly," I said. "Velma, you take Shaggy and Scooby downstairs. Daphne and I will look around upstairs."

Shaggy, Scooby, and Velma walked downstairs and through a door. They told us later that the hallway was lined with big pictures of smiling people eating Yummy Foods products.

"Man, it's a little hard to walk down this hall with all these people looking at us," Shaggy complained.

"They're just pictures, Shaggy," Velma said.

"Maybe to you," Shaggy said. "But to

Scooby and me they're re-
minders of how hungry
we are."

Suddenly, they heard
a growling sound echo
through the hallway.

"See what I mean?"
Shaggy said to Velma.
"Scooby's so hungry his
stomach is growling."

"Either that, or Mr.
Hyde is around here somewhere," Velma
said.

"Like, I sure hope not! What exactly are
we looking for, Velma?" asked Shaggy.

"The food production line," she replied. "If
Mr. Hyde is really going to add his secret ingredient, that's where he'll be heading."

Just ahead, they saw another door that
was slightly open. Velma took a closer look.

"It's the food lab," she said. "And take a
look at this!"

"Like, that's a doorknob, Velma," Shaggy
said.

"I know it's a doorknob," Velma replied. "Look what's in it."

Shaggy and Scooby took a closer look.

"Like, I don't know what you're talking about, Velma," Shaggy said. "All I see is a plain old doorknob with key on a big ring of keys in the lock and orange powder on it."

"It's a clue, Shaggy," Velma said. "And I have a hunch that if Mr. Hyde left these keys here, he'll be back to get them. Let's go find Fred and Daphne, quick."

"Who's out there?" came a voice from inside the room. Before they could run away, the door opened.

"Wally Nebbins!" Velma cried out.

"What's going on?" he asked.

"We're looking for Mr. —" Shaggy began, but Velma put her hand over his mouth to stop him.

"— Dr. Jenkins," Velma finished Shaggy's sentence. "Have you seen him?"

"No, and that's fine by me," Wally replied.

"Sorry to disturb you," Velma said. "We'll

see you later." Wally Nebbins closed the door.

"Whew, that was close," Velma said.

"Like, why did you stop me?" Shaggy asked.

"Because — as far as I'm concerned — Wally Nebbins is a suspect. He's angry at Dr. Jenkins, remember? And now we've found him in a place where he might be up to no good."

"Wow! Like, you're right," Shaggy agreed.

"Now let's go find Fred and Daphne and show them the clue," Velma said. She carefully took the key out of the lock and put the whole key ring in her pocket. The three of them started back down the hall. Shaggy and Scooby followed but stopped when something caught their eye.

"First, a free taste of Yummaroni and Cheese, and now this," Shaggy sighed. "Scoob, this must be our lucky day."

"Rou-bet!" Scooby agreed.

Shaggy and Scooby stood in front of a Yummy Foods display with a FREE SAMPLES sign on it. They started pulling items off the shelves and munched to their stomach's content.

"How about a little something in case we get hungry later?" Shaggy asked.

As he and Scooby filled their arms with goodies, a growling sound echoed through the hallway.

"If you're hungry, Scoob, have another snack," Shaggy said.

"Rat rasn't ree," Scooby said.

The growling got louder.

"Well, if it wasn't you, and it wasn't me, what could it be?" Shaggy said.

The growling sounded like it was coming from right behind them. Shaggy and Scooby looked at each other.

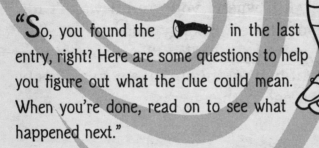

"So, you found the ⚲ in the last entry, right? Here are some questions to help you figure out what the clue could mean. When you're done, read on to see what happened next."

1. What is the clue?

2. What does the clue have to do with the mystery?

3. Which of the suspects could have left this clue?

Clue Keeper Entry 6

"Mr. Hyde!" Shaggy screamed.

"*Rikes!*" Scooby yelled.

They dropped their goodies and ran as Mr. Hyde chased them down the hallway.

"*Relp!*" yelled Scooby as he and Shaggy ran down the hallway. Mr. Hyde was still chasing them, but the growling started getting softer and softer.

"Start trying doors, Scoob," Shaggy called. "There's gotta be a place to hide around here somewhere." Shaggy kept tugging on doorknobs. Finally, an unmarked door swung open.

"Quick! In here, Scoob," Shaggy instructed. He and Scooby ran inside and slammed the door shut behind them. It was completely dark inside.

"Now don't make any noise, Scooby," Shaggy whispered. "With any luck, we'll be able to save our hide and hide from Mr. Hyde."

Shaggy heard a muffled yell.

"Uh-oh," Shaggy whispered. "I don't think we're alone in here. Let's go!"

"Rhat rabout Rister Ryde?" asked Scooby.

"I'm more afraid of a monster I *can't* see than one I can," Shaggy replied.

Shaggy opened the door a crack. "Ready, Scoob? One. Two. Three. Ahhhhhhhh!" He flung open the door and the two of them ran out into the hallway.

They were halfway down the hall when they realized it was empty.

"Hey, I guess we fooled that creepy Mr. Hyde after all," Shaggy said with a grin. Then he froze.

The muffled moaning sound he'd heard before filled the hallway. But this time, there was also a thumping noise, like something banging against the floor.

"Zoinks!" Shaggy exclaimed. "That thing's still in there. And it sounds like it's coming our way."

"Relp!" Scooby yelled.

Daphne, Velma, and I were looking for Shaggy and Scooby when we heard Scooby's voice. We ran through the hallways, following Scooby's yells. We found them standing in the hallway in front of an open door.

"Are you two all right?" I asked.

"We're fine, Fred," Shaggy replied. "But I'm not too sure about Dr. Jenkins."

"What do you mean?" asked Velma.

"Take a look," Shaggy said, pointing into the closet. We ran over and saw Dr. Jenkins at the back of the closet. He was tied to a chair and had tape over his mouth. We carefully removed the tape and untied him.

"Whew!" he said, rubbing his sore wrists. "Thanks, kids. I thought no one was going to find me."

"I'm glad we did, Dr. Jenkins," I said. "Because that means that Mr. Hyde is really a phony."

"And that his so-called secret ingredient is harmless," Velma added.

"Except that it will change the food's color," Dr. Jenkins said. "I won't be able to sell Yummaroni and Cheese if it's not the right color."

"I'll bet we could stop him if we only knew who he was," Daphne said.

"Here's something that may help," Dr. Jenkins said. "I grabbed it from Mr. Hyde as he pushed me through the trap door under the stage." He held out a piece of white fabric.

"May I see that, Dr. Jenkins?" Velma asked. She took a closer look and her nose twitched. "I have a hunch that our little game of 'Hyde-and-seek' is just about over."

I examined the white fabric and noticed a peculiar smell.

"Velma's right," I agreed. "It's time to set a trap."

"Zoinks! Did you see the  on page 46? Open up your Clue Keeper, grab your pen or pencil, and answer these questions about it."

1. What is the clue?

2. Where have you seen something like this before?

3. Which of the suspects could have left this clue?

"Keep on reading now to see how we tried to catch Mr. Hyde."

48

Clue Keeper Entry 7

"Once Mr. Hyde finds out we've found Dr. Jenkins, he'll want to ruin the entire batch of Yummaroni and Cheese," I said. "If we're going to capture him, we need to act fast."

"Where's the food production line?" asked Velma.

"It's just down the hall and to the right," Dr. Jenkins said.

"Can you show us the best place to hide in there?" I asked.

"No problem," he said. "There's even a walk-in food locker we can use to hold him once we capture him."

"That's great," I replied. "While you're showing us where to hide, Shaggy and Scooby will be ready to distract him."

"Like, I think we've distracted Mr. Hyde from his work enough for one day," Shaggy said. "Don't you, Scoob?"

"Rabsolutely!" agreed Scooby.

"Does that mean you won't help us, Scooby?" Daphne asked.

"Ruh-uh," Scooby said, shaking his head.

"Not even for a Scooby Snack?" asked Velma.

"Rell . . ." said Scooby, thinking. *"Rokay."*

Velma tossed him the Scooby Snack and Scooby gobbled it down.

"Like, what about me?" Shaggy asked. "I never get snacks for helping."

"How about a bag of Yummy Crunchies?" offered Dr. Jenkins.

Shaggy's eyes lit up. "Sold!" he announced.

We followed Dr. Jenkins to the production line room. He unlocked the door and left it slightly open so Mr. Hyde could get in.

"Jinkies!" gasped Velma.

"This is where our automated equipment measures, mixes, cooks, condenses, and packages the food," Dr. Jenkins explained.

The room was filled with the biggest pieces of mechanical equipment we'd ever seen. Boxlike machines with mechanical arms hung from a track along the ceiling. Metal racks, circular platters, mixing blades, and other things stuck out every which way. A conveyor belt snaked its way all over the room, in and out of various machines.

"If he's going to put anything into the food, it will be over here," Dr. Jenkins said. He pointed to a row of huge, shiny stainless

steel vats. Metal ladders reached to the top of each vat. "The food locker is over there, and we can hide behind the control platform right next to it."

"Shaggy and Scooby, you wait by the vats," I said. "When Mr. Hyde comes in, get him to chase you over here. Then we'll push him into the food locker."

Shaggy and Scooby walked back to the area in front of the vats.

Suddenly, we all heard Mr. Hyde's famil-

iar growl. Shaggy and Scooby ducked behind one of the vats. Mr. Hyde slowly approached. He looked around and then started climbing one of the ladders.

Shaggy and Scooby came out from behind the vat wearing white lab coats.

"Like, excuse me," Shaggy said. "I am Dr. Shaggy and this is my associate, Dr. Scooby. We're from the food police, and we need to give you a ticket for putting unauthorized ingredients into the Yummaroni and Cheese."

Mr. Hyde looked puzzled, then he let out a mighty roar and jumped off the ladder.

"Zoinks!" Shaggy yelled. "Okay, we'll let you off with a warning this time. Gotta run! Let's go, Scoob!"

Shaggy and Scooby started running toward the food locker with Mr. Hyde close behind.

"Get ready, Freddy!" Shaggy yelled. Scooby ran by first. We jumped up, but instead of seeing Mr. Hyde, we grabbed Shaggy by mistake and pushed him into the locker. Mr. Hyde kept chasing Scooby.

"Relp! Raggy! Red! Raphne! Relma!" Scooby yelled. He climbed up one of the ladders and jumped onto a nearby conveyor belt. Mr. Hyde followed Scooby. Just as he was reaching out to grab Scooby's tail, Scooby jumped off and landed right on the control panel.

The machinery suddenly sprang to life and the production line kicked into high gear. Before Mr. Hyde could jump off, one of the mechanical arms reached out and grabbed him. Mr. Hyde started screaming.

"Help! Help me!" he yelled.

Dr. Jenkins turned off the control panel. The mechanical arm dumped Mr. Hyde into one of the vats.

"Now let's see who this Mr. Hyde really is," Dr. Jenkins said.

"**H**ere we go, mate," the waiter says. "Fish and chips, all around." He places baskets of fish and chips on the table for us.

"Like, excuse me," Shaggy says. "But you left someone's newspaper in my lunch."

"That's the way they serve it, Shaggy," Velma explains. "It's very British."

Scooby starts giggling.

"What's so funny, Scoob?" asks Shaggy.

"*Romics!*" answers Scooby, reading the comic strips on the newspapers in his basket.

"While they're reading the funnies, how

about solving the mystery?" Daphne says to you.

"You've got all the information you need in your Clue Keeper," Velma adds. "Remember, take a look at your suspects. Then compare them with the clues you found. Figure out who couldn't have done it. Think about which suspect all the clues point to."

Daphne smiles at you. "I'll bet you figure out who was pretending to be Mr. Hyde in no time."

You begin thinking hard. Who could it be?

"Turn the page when you think you know who was pretending to be Mr. Hyde!"

"It was Izzy Fenwick!" Fred says. "As you probably guessed, right?"

"It was clear from the beginning that a lot of people didn't want Yummaroni and Cheese to be a success," Daphne says. "There was Wally Nebbins, who was angry about not getting credit for the secret ingredient."

"And Izzy Fenwick, who hated cleaning up the cheesy messes," Velma continues. "And Katherine Tatum, the head of So-Good Foods."

"They each had their reasons, but not all

of them could have left all three clues," Fred explains.

"Only two people had the special red-and-yellow pen we found behind the podium," Daphne says. "Remember? Dr. Jenkins only had two, and he gave one to Izzy Fenwick. K. J. Tatum took the other."

"So that made them our first suspects," Velma says. "But then we found the keys that Mr. Hyde left in the door. Only two of the suspects could have had those keys."

"Wally Nebbins, who worked in the lab was one of them, and Izzy Fenwick was the other," Fred says. "Izzy was the janitor, remember? That means he had keys to all the rooms in the building so he could clean up."

"But the last clue made it clear that Izzy was our man," Daphne says.

"That's right," Fred adds. "Wally Nebbins had a white handkerchief and wore a white lab coat, so the piece of fabric Dr. Jenkins had could have come from him."

"But when I examined the fabric, my nose twitched because it smelled," Velma says. "It smelled of vinegar. And Izzy used a white

rag to wipe the vinegar off Scooby's back, remember?"

"All of the clues pointed to Izzy Fenwick," Fred says.

"By the way, Izzy didn't really have any Mr. Hyde potion to put into the Yummaroni and Cheese," Daphne adds. "It was just food coloring. He was pretending so he could scare everyone."

"And it almost worked, too," Velma says. "Until Scooby-Doo saved the day."

"We're really glad you came today," Daphne says. "We hope we'll see you again soon."

"Like, not just soon," Shaggy says.

"Rooby-rooby-rooooooon!" Scooby shouts.